BUMBLEBEE PUBLISHING
I HOPE LOVE WILL MAKE US AGAIN

Prabhaharan was born in 2000 in a family that has agriculture as its backbone. He is living with his family in Coimbatore, Tamil Nadu. This book is his debut novel as a writer. He is passionate about writing since his school years. He is doing his first degree in physics and dreams of becoming a good writer.

Get in touch with him below:
Instagram – @just_a_happiest_being
Facebook – @prabhaharan

I HOPE LOVE WILL MAKE US AGAIN

PRABHAHARAN MANOHARAN

Published by Bumblebee Publishing
An imprint of Shree Balaji International
59, N S Road, 3rd Floor, Room No. 15B,
Kolkata, West Bengal – 700 001
Email: editorialbumblebee@gmail.com

I Hope Love Will Make Us Again
Copyright © Prabhaharan Manoharan, 2021

ISBN Print Book – 978-81-949485-2-0

*To all the lovely heart,
I crossed.*

Chapter 1

It is a rainy day – there is heavy traffic due to the fall of a container in the middle of the road – and I am getting late for my music class. It is my 5th month of learning music and playing the violin. Finally, it takes the police around 30 minutes to make clear the way.

I reached the class with wet clothes. My hair and even on my mobile phone screen were soaked in water. My good luck is that the music teacher also had some work and informed all that he will be late for half an hour.

Everybody in the class is chatting to one another, and some people are playing the old notes. For me, the class begins only when the rain stops and the music teacher arrives.

The name of my music teacher is John. He knows

to play many musical instruments. I have grown in the orphanage until I completed my studies. After I completed my studies, John sir took care of me financially and encouraged my musical skill. John sir is famous. He makes quite a few album songs with international celebrities. However, no one believes that he had done the album with the stars because of his simplicity. He just wears stitched clothes and puts a very old model framed glass to his eyes. But the worst part of him is that we can't judge his moods. We don't know when he will get angry, and we also don't know when he will laugh.

It looks like that the rain is not going to stop anytime soon. So everybody actually has gone to have a cup of tea in the bakery, which is just on the down floor.

I, too, want to go to that bakery. But I hate regular tea. I love lemon tea which is a speciality at that bakery. Now I don't have the mood to drink that.

I have only one friend in the class. He is absent today, and I'm not familiar with anyone as I am an introvert. So, I just come out to the balcony and look over the rain, sky, black clouds and the rainbow. Actually, there are two rainbows.

I remember one of my friends told me how the rainbow is formed. It's fascinating when the sun rays strike on the raindrop, it gets reflected on the sky, and it leads to the beautiful rainbow.

Suddenly, there is a gentle smooth sound of 'Hello' by a sweet voice. I turned with wonder because of that voice. There is a rainbow. Oh! No, it is a girl with beauty who can win all the world beauties. She asks me something, but I forget all the reality as my eyes make my soul freeze by looking at her eyes.

You don't know about her eyes. But don't worry, I will tell. But how much can I talk about that infinity beauty? Her eyes had a charcoal-coloured eyeball with a diamond of brightness. Eyebrows are just a black coloured low stretched rainbow. But, then, her eyelids are soft like a flower—totally like a butterfly flapping its wing when she blinks her eyes.

It is just only her eyes. If I explain her full beauty. You may come in search of her, and so I stop it here. But in short, she is a soulful sculpture made by angels.

She waves her hand before my face to bring me back to the reality from the world of her beauty. I said, "Sorry… What?"

She asks, "Is it the music class run by John sir?"

I said, "Yes, it is."

She said "Thank you" and went inside

Again, I looked at the rainbow; I feel like it's losing its brightness.

Chapter 2

Last night was full of her dreams. I could hardly sleep, as she kept walking in my eyes with the same soul-stealing eyes.

Today, I came as early as I could. I searched for her in that big hall. But she wasn't there. She must be late. John sir also hadn't come till now.

There was a familiar sound of his old model car, and I figured that John sir had arrived. Everybody became serious. They lost their smile and faked strictness on their face. Everybody, along with me, took positions with our respective violins.

John sir come and stand at the middle of the stage and say "Good evening".

Suddenly, the same sweet sound of yesterday says, "Excuse me, sir".

John sir asked her to get in by just waving his hands. She comes inside; the entire hall is filled with people, but there are still quite a few empty seats. She comes towards me and takes a seat near me.

You can't feel the feeling I felt at this time. And I, too, can't put that feeling in words.

The worlds most beautiful girl coming and sitting near this flaw. I can't concentrate on anything but only on her. I can't hear the words coming out of John, but I can listen to her silence.

I come back to reality when everybody starts to play the violin. Everybody plays Vivaldi's Winter season, which I can play without looking at anything. In fact, I can play it correctly in my dreams too. She also plays along with all. I think she must have learnt to play the violin somewhere before.

John sir wave his hand as the music goes down and up.

Everything goes well; I play the music along with seeing her beauty. I feel the music have some more pleasure today.

Suddenly, one of her strings gets broken. She becomes too nervous. I think she is too sensitive because there are small tears in her eyes because of the broken strings. I feel like the sky is broken when I find her sad.

And without hesitation, I give her a violin which is spare of my friend. My friend is not too perfect in playing the violin but good at bringing an extra as his violin usually does not make a good rhythm.

● ● ●

As I give the violin, my friend looks at me like, "Who the hell you are, man?". I never mind him.

She has tears but also a smile and happiness on her face. She looked at me for some times. But I feel shy to look at her face and tried to focus on music, I think.

After the class is over, she comes and says, "Thank you so much". I said, "No mention". My inner thoughts are jumping up and down, telling me to ask for her number.

She continued, "I want to repair my violin". Can you show me the right place to do that? "Actually, I am new here.'

I said, "Okay, sure, if it is not a problem, I will take care of your violin".

She thinks something and said, "Okay... no problem... and may I have your number?"

I have felt like the entire light of the universe is glowing inside me, but I make sure to not show it on my face. I give her my number, and I get her number too. Along with my violin, I take her violin for repair.

In the evening, I hold her violin, but it feels like having herself in my room. And then, I fixed the broken string in her violin. So, I start to play in it. I play Pirates of the Caribbean theme, Slumdog Millionaire theme, and finally, again and again, I play the music of Titanic.

Chapter 3

The next day, when I gave her the violin, she thanked me. She asks, "How much?" I don't know what to tell. I just stayed silent.

I tell her, "I fixed it myself, so no problem". She smiled.

John comes in as he had a notice in his hand. He hands it over to me to pass it to everyone. I passed it to everyone without reading the information. Last, I looked over it, it is a notice about a music competition this year. I have really waited for this kind of chance.

John sir says, "In this competition, you can play any musical instruments as a solo, duo or even as a band beat. I need all people to join". After he stops, there is a slight noise of chatting filled over the entire hall. John sir ask for silence and begin to end his session of today's class as soon as possible.

Today the class held only for 15 minutes or less than that. Then, after John went, everybody begins to go.

I realize that I have rarely looked at her today. I packed my violin and moved up to the entrance. She calls me with her sweet voice.

There I feel how much beauty my name had. I turn back with a smile of excitement.

She said, "I have to ask you something".

My brain begins to fill with suspense but does not show that in my eyes and face; I say "yes…"

She said, "I too want to participate in that competition. I know to play the guitar. If it is possible, and if you wish, can we participate as a duo?

It's really like a cluster of stars falling into my hands. I actually want to thank God for this. I said, "Yes… It's my pleasure".

She smiled, and my soul jumped up to the clouds and touches the blue sky.

I tell her, "I make the music and make you join". And we dispersed with a smile.

I reached my room. I switched off my phone. I emptied my room. And I locked my door, windows and thought of everything. I closed my eyes and looked at her eyes at a touching distance. And I open my eyes, I take my old guitar and piano. I placed the piano in the center of my room. Already the space is empty. Now the piano is at the center, the guitar on my hand and the imaginary version of her. I start to compose a piece of music with that all.

I composed it entirely for a duration of 4:00 minutes. I played that music again and again without a break. I record it on my mobile phone and send it to her.

Within 5 minutes, she called me, it is really dark nighttime. She also feels the music exactly as I feel it. She thanked me for making such a wonder. I feel like the intensity of that music get denser in me after she speaks with me.

After that we chat, speak with many laughs, shy, little love and more about music. Then, we begin to practice the music. She adds a small measure of ballad dance to our performance.

The days are becoming lightning when we together for practice. At night she becomes a significant hurdle to sleep. In the night, I smile and smile on thinking about the daytime which has gone with her.

One day, while lying on the terrace and looking at the black sky with curved Moon and stars. I said to myself, "Yaa maybe! I think", with a smile. I ask myself, "Because I feel I need her every second near me, holding the hands and looking at the beauty in the world".

After that, there are no answers as there is no question from myself to ask me. I begin to sleep with seeing her beautiful face in the entire sky.

Chapter 4

It is the day of the competition. We entered before the event started. I looked over the hall. The hall is filled with a heavy population of people and musical instruments, but above all, the constant noise. Correctly after half an hour, the event starts. We are numbered as fifth to play. I looked at her. She was a little nervous. She also looked at me with that shivering face. I ask her, "what?" with a smile. She answers, "little fear arousing in me". I smiled again. I tell her, "no problem, I will take care of everything". I hug her to give hope. She looked at me and say "I believe you," with hopeful eyes.

The first competitor was a duo like us. One played the violin, while the other played the piano. The heavy noise becomes silent by their music. They make the entire hall drown in their melody sea. After they complete, we applaud them with the noise of clapping.

The next one was a solo performer. He played dazzling music. The other played a melody again. Unfortunately, it was not good enough to hear. I think he must be a beginner.

After a while, it becomes our turn to accommodate the stage. We go there. I checked the time once again. All was good, remarkably the light that travelling along with us.

I sit in the chair, which is centred at the stage. She puts the guitar in her knee while I made her sit on my knee. Her ears and her face, entirely she was close to me. I put my hands on the strings e, a, d while she concentrates her hands on the strings g, b, e. My other hand goes over d, d#, c, e, e# while her fingers move on a, a#, b#, b. We played it as we had practised. She enjoys the music or maybe my closeness. She presents her face with a broad smile.

I enjoyed both the music and her happiness. I didn't want to end this session. I want to be like this for my entire lifetime. I want her closeness and the presence of music on us. But we end as we planned and practice. I walked back along with not taking my eyes from her glowing face. I can't even get the applaud from the hall. I go back and sit in my place near her like someone has taken my conscience.

The rest of the day is gone by seeing her face, smile, eyes, and the look she gave towards me.

They give the prize in different categories like melody, rock and so on. We win for melody. She was surprised when they announce our name for the award.

After it was all completed, we come out with the prize. It was raining. We don't know when the rain began as the acoustic of the hall was soundproof. I call John sir to tell him this sweet news, but he did not pick up; maybe he was busy. We both entered a restaurant. We buy a burger and a coke. We eat along with speaking about the competition. She thanked me for making all this possible. I rarely speak. I mostly looked at her facial expressions more than hearing her words.

She bends her smooth hands into her leather hand back. And it comes back with a gift box. She hands it over to me. I surprisingly looked at her. She says, "I bought it. And think to give it, if we win." with a glowing smile, "And so take it, it is for you."

I smiled. I take that but did not open it. She also did not mind that; maybe she wants me to open it in her absence.

I rushed from there just to open that box soon. It was a sculpture of a musician with a green plant behind; and the violin before him. The entire sculpture is framed inside an uncompleted heart.

I kept staring at that in the moonlight while lying on the terrace.

Chapter 5

It is another cloudy day. It is also early morning. I have not been able to sleep as my mind is thinking about the return gift to give her. I think of buying a statue as same as her or of purchasing something like books. But I want to give her something more connected with me. So finally, I decided to give her an old Indian currency of ten rupees. That ten-rupee has been with me for a long time. And I believe that it was given to me by some people who have a blood relationship with me.

I was astonished that I was giving her this precious part of my life. I cleaned the dirtiness from my body. I looked at the mirror again and again. I feel like the beauty percentage of me have increased. I comb my hair continuously until it becomes stylish.

I called her through mobile, but she did not respond. I think she hardly has time to spend with her mobile. Anyway, I hurry to cross my path toward the class.

I was the first in the class as usual. I look for her as keeping my eyes on the entrance door. Slowly, the crowd keep filling the hall one by one.

She was keeping me thrilled by delaying her presence. She comes after the hall has filled. She was the last one to come. I became a little more nervous. Finally, she seated herself with a bright glowing smile towards me. She was still in the glow as the first time I saw her. She was magic.

John sir come. The class begins. Everybody engages with their violins, but I am engaged in staring at her. I lowered my head on the strings of the violin and looked at her eyes. She was like a calm flower but playing the game of creating Strom inside me. Everybody playing, and I was playing something wrong as enough to sense by that music devil. He shouted to stop. He asks me to go out as my mental presence was hanged with the druggie eyes of her. I got out from there.

I wait outside at the café opposite the class. I waited by looking at her through the window. The window with a beautiful frame enhances her beauty too. She looked at me occasionally. Every time she looked at me and find I was looking at her and kissing my heart for her. I made her aware that I was waiting for her to come through sign language. Her face becomes bright with the broad, killing smile.

The class ends everybody gone. She comes towards me as increasing my fight, flight hormone. I looked at her as a statue in the small café. She asked me, "what?" not through words but by raising her eyebrow with the same killing smile.

I respond just with a smile and hand over the coffee which I bought for her. She sipped as throwing her eyes at me. Every time she was near, it been like my whole happiness is there along with me, speaking with me, smiling with me, and so on.

My heart is oscillating in thinking about the gift to give her. As she completes her coffee, the oscillation becomes heavier, more profound and something weight fill in the cell of my heart. I pay the bill after.

We walk along the road. She was quiet and waiting for me to tell the matter. We smiled at each other. I give her the gift. At first, she thought that it was for the coffee. I tell her the secret and the reason behind handing the money. She was surprised. She becomes a glow in the middle of the road.

I come home. I played the music played with the playlist of love songs. I danced without synchronizing to the tune. I love that evening. I love that day. I love that road. I love that coffee shop. And I love that girl with an enormous quantity. My mobile ringed. I want it to be her, and it was her.

She asked me why I have given the money that was connected to me so much. I know the reason behind it. But I say something to deviate her from her guess. I tell her that many people give me their money or coin as a gift of their presence in my life. Also, add that it was the first time I give such a thing.

She smiled with enough sound for me to hear. But, then, for a long time, we did not talk and celebrated the invisible connection and peaceful conversation.

Chapter 6

I woke up with the dream of holding her hand. I hurried to class with the thoughts of her. I was humming the old love song along with thinking about meeting her in the class. The ride is not similar to before when she was not in my life.

There are already some people who occupied little of the entire room. I just get into the hall with a silent smile inside my head. I was looking over everybody. There is another pair in our class. They are trying to play the violin like we did in the competition. As supporting my head on the desk, l looked over them. They were the beautiful couple I had seen. But it was not felt like that. I just close my eyes and looked at my soul breaking smiling face of her. As in the same state, I take my violin and play it. The play goes for nearly five minutes, also the lighting of her face inside the clouds of my head. In simple, I was transferring her thoughts into the soul through the violin and bow.

I only opened my eyes when the thoughts of her break to bring me to be neutral. I looked around. Everybody was looking at me. Everybody's face was stunned. It takes few seconds for them to believe that my music of mine has stopped. After they believed the truth, they all clapped.

I feel timid. I moaned thank you with my lips. I know everybody knows only the music, not its birth. Even she, who was the reason for the music, will never know the birthplace or it born through my mind. Everybody comes towards me and tell me how the music made them feel.

I was looking for her to come at perfectly now. But she was not coming. After hearing the sound of John sir's drastic car sound, everybody flies to their place. My heart is beating again and again as it is looking for her presence. There is a lot of emotions eating my mind. I was constantly staring at the entrance door. But she was not coming. Instead, John sir comes into the class or hall.

Everybody takes their violin, and John sir begin to teach us. Still, my heart is looking to engage with her. I pray for her not to miss this class. I thought that she must have missed her taxi, or she had some problem. I couldn't concentrate on the class.

Her absence made me sick. It was like the whole

world is breaking and fell like rain into my heart. Even not a single word of anyone in the hall wasn't getting into my mind. I actually hate the feel which I am feeling, but I can't stop.

I couldn't get anything don't till the end of the class, arriving at the house. It all vanished in the tragedy of her absence. I call to her after a heavy hesitation. The call is ringing continuously, but no one picked up. I tried again and again. The hesitation faded as no one pick the call. My heart was begging for her heart to pick the call and explain the reason for her absence.

I have nearly called more than five times. After that, no ring but a computer voice was telling her mobile got switched off.

Chapter 7

The last night I sleep very late after that bad feeling. So I get up too late. The first thing that comes to mind is to call her and enquire about her absence. I called her, but her phone was still switched off. I feel too bad. That creates a fear that today also she won't come.

I was on my way to the class. I drive fastly to get excited by her presence. Afterwards, slow down my speed in order not to get a bad feeling like yesterday.

I was the first person to get to the hall. I sense someone was coming up the staircase. All the cells are crying it to be her but not. It was my fellow classmate. I just cut her conversation with the sign language of shopping head. There was a sound of a group of both girls and boys coming up the staircase. Again the heart, brain and mostly all of mine are begging for her presence in that group. Again my feeling gets cheated by itself.

I hate myself for expecting her and getting the feeling of looser. I pull my headset in the ears and play my favourite song of *"chaiya chaiya"*. So as to make my feeling more suppressed, I increase the volume, although my mobile warns me not to do that. And the song of my playlist in the shuffle mood. I closed my eyes. But the feeling about her arises in between the musical notes of the songs. I try to concentrate on the music more than than the thoughts about her.

Above the song or music playing in my ears. I can also sense the hall filling with people. I open my eyes after a while. I looked at the blurred vision of the window. Someone was coming. I try not to think anything, so I put myself into others near me. Then, without my awareness, I looked at the entrance. And surprising, it was her. Yes, it was her with the glowing face. Just like the first time, I was looking at her and becoming like water in the freezer. She was coming towards me with a smiling face and waving a hi to me. She was coming, and the music was playing. It was like magic happening.

She just sits next to me. I don't know how to tell her that I have missed her or have tried to reach her. I want her to know what in my mind without my words. But also, I know it won't happen. But if it happens everybody will be happier, without concerning others or with regarding others. So my heart is telling me, "hold her she was the one made for you".

It feels something uneasy to look at her eyes. But in the meantime, I could learn that she was looking at me with infinitesimal intervals. I want her to feel the same way I was feeling for her. John sir come nearly more than fifteen minutes. Between that, I won't speak with her anything though I have millions of things to talk to her about. Mostly I want to tell her I want her presence in every day of life. She has an importance in my life as much as I had.

While John sir putting his knowledge of music into us, I and she looked at each other without showing that to others. At one time, of that coincidental look of each other, she smiled at me. The beautifully killing smile. It was like thousands and thousands of flowers blooming simultaneously. I reciprocate the smile to her. We both really struggle to concentrate on the class that going on.

After the class have wind-up. As packing our stuff, we begin the conversation nervously. I enquired about her absence. She said, "my father has ALS. He became serious yesterday morning. And we rushed to hospital and still he was there. I asked, "Is he okay now?" She replied, "yes, he was. Is okay. But he was under observation for today".

She never talks about the call I made. And I too. After some diverted talks, she left me. I have not yet told her about the love I had for her or the yesterday feeling about her. I rush to get her.

Chapter 8

I missed telling her about the love I had for her. But I was strongly determined to say to her today. I have a strong feeling that she will throw a positive response into my heart. I was continuously preparing to tell her about my love. I was constantly rearranging the phrases that shout out my feeling of love for her. I try to make it simple more and more. All the love scenes of various movies are glittering in some part of my mind.

I was delaying the class by looking again and again at the face of mine in the mirror. I comb my hair to make them neat, or at least not with a sour look. I was becoming crazy on thinking that I was going to become committed. So I never make a rush in today's ride. I make it smooth and completely travel of feeling the love.

I stepped into the hall. It was the same as yesterday, but it became special for me today. I sit in the middle of the hall. I had the feeling of her presence in intangible form. I play my violin with a heart full of love for her.

I want her presence soon. I want to explore all the love that filled in my heart like a book full of flowers. I want to have her as my soul and not a soulmate or part of my soul. I want to walk on the side of the beach as holding her hands. I want to kiss her, hug her and smile, laugh.

I was playing the violin as being in a dream. I stopped playing the music as I hear someone was coming. After some people arrived, I looked at the sky through the window. The atmosphere is partially filled with rainy clouds. I was thinking about the event that was about to happen. It was going to be a totally life-changing event for me.

I have not changed my position or looking at the sky with rainy clouds, though they all come. I looked around. Precisely at the exact moment, John sir enter the class. He seems angry. His angry face made me fear that he must come to know my love feeling for her. He starts to take the class. But mostly, he leaves us all alone and makes himself alone. His face reveals he had some problem and not reveal what the problem is. I looked around for her, but she was not there. I thought she was sitting at the first bench like hidden from my sight. But she was not even in the first row. I searched again and again for her. I, again and again, rechecked every face. I cheated myself again. I go nearly to the feeling of crying. My face also becomes like John sir's, which goes through the problem but can't express to anyone. It starts to rain. And it was the first time I hate the rain too deeply. It was like the clouds crying instead for my eyes. John sir and I were not speaking anything till the rain stop. He says 'leave!" after the clouds stop raining. Everybody leaves. I leave the hall too with a heart of wound. I walked down to the road. It becomes the first day for me to feel blessed to have my eyes. I looked at the coffee shop with her presence. She has wet hair. She was playing with the water, which was put down by the clouds.

My legs pulled me to her. She was smiling at me. She hands me lemon tea. It was again like magic. A lovely melody song play in that coffee shop enhanced the favour of the time. I am falling in love with her, again and again, every second. She says, " It becomes late and rainy. And so I can't attend the class today". Actually, I have to thank rain, if it not come, the present feeling of mine will not come today for me. I nod my head as a response to her statement. She plays with the rain. And I was thinking about how to tell the love. I promise myself I will say to it after the last sip. I make a slow sip once and a fast one next. And it continued like that, as I promise, I get ready to put my love in the form of words to her. I called. She turns back with a smiling face and few drops of rainwater, increasing the intensity of her beauty. I make my face serious; I looked at her eyes. "I am in love with you. Just think and say you answer". Her face becomes stunned. I walked away with a smiling face though it's raining. After a short distance, I turn back and tell her, "I know you love me. Tell me soon, don't delay it", very loudly and mainly with a smiling face.

Chapter 9

I look for a message from her, something that offends me or something that's making sense that she also loves me. But she was silent with no words. I want to look at her face and need to decide what she was thinking about me. So I was being in a lot of confusion that was completely eating my peace.

As usual, she comes to the class. But she was not looking the same as her yesterday. She never looked at me, not at least once. I constantly looked at her while John sir was happily talking about some old stuff. I wanted her to look at me at least once a time. But she was hiding her face from me. She was also hiding all her feelings.

Myself is telling me, "You made a mistake by confessing about your love. If you do not tell her about the love, at least she will be a good friend. But you ruined all." I, too, feel that though the wordings of myself is hurting, it is true. I was the one who ruined everything between her and me. If I haven't put my love in the format of words, she will look at me, and nothing will be odd.

I want yesterday to completely vanish from both of our life. At least I have to change something in the events of yesterday. But it all will not happen. I feel awkward, shameful to look at her face.

I am hurting myself by telling me, again and again, I was the mistake. I, too, feel the same and am unable to look at her. I want to fix this. But I don't know how to fix it.

I was constantly staring at her as I was thinking to fix the problem. At that time, she turned to me. I looked at her make a tiny smile which conveying both happy and sad feelings. Her face was stiff. She doesn't show any emotion except some kind of avoidance for me. She turned very soon.

I was confused again in infinity amount. I don't know why she looked. What she had on her mind while looked at me.

Nearly my heart feels like all the hope of my life is ruining. I was looking at her with a face of tragedy. Whenever others look at me, I make a false smiling facing. I want to beg her not to be like this with me as it is like pulling out my soul from my heart.

The class ends, which I can sense after few minutes. Everybody was packing their things and

• • •

escaping from the hall. I was sitting at the centre like an old statue and constantly looking for her look at me.

She also packing her things. I was looking at her as usual of this day. She looked at me once again, but it lasts only a few seconds. I can't even put that she had seen me with great assurance. Then, she exits the hall. I shout her name to stop. She stopped at the veranda. I rush my body towards her. Tears start coming out of my eyes.

She looked at me. She makes her eyes with stretches that show she had some irritation or some problem. That makes me more down. Then, finally, she nods her head to ask me, "what?". I don't know what to tell. I just stand blankly with empty words.

She continues to move away as I am standing there. After a few more steps, she turned back and said that "I want some days to think." It becomes a form of great joy and glows like sunlight. To increase the conversation, I asked her, "but why?". She replied without turning back, "because it's about the whole life of mine and yours too. I don't know whether you could sustain with me or not", with a smile that I couldn't see. I laughed and put "my angel, I will sustain with you, though you want to kill. But don't leave me". She has long gone away from me, but she can hear what I said. She replied, "let see tomorrow."

I drag myself back to my home. It becomes dark in the sky and everywhere in the world, especially at the terrace of my house. I set the moving light at the deck and looking at the sky along with the melody playlist. I was thinking about her and the conversation I had with her. I believed "If someone does not need the thing, they with tell don't need, but if they want it, they have to think for it" and so "she needs me, and she was thinking for me". This clever thought of mine made me smile like a madman. As the ideas flow over, I was falling asleep. As good sleep comes to me, it was disturbed by the ringing sound of my mobile phone. It was her. I can't believe my eyes. It is like a dream. I picked up the call. She said melodically, "hello". I tell back it after a struck. My face is smiling as sensing that she would say something that will make my everyday life a celebration. And she did that as I thought. And it is love.

Chapter 10

Love is always a magical feeling. It makes you more narcissistic. It creates an unaware illusion that you two are the only beings in the world, and everything else fades away. You always feel the presence of the other, though you're in a conscious mind. And it all the magic held by the world's most beautiful feeling – The Love.

We begin to love each other. We try to teach each other to love more. I know we can't completely love anyone or completely hate anyone. We all love only a minimum part of anyone and hate the balance. But I am telling or writing to you that I completely love her. She creates the feeling that my days should be a surrounding of her, and that's all that my birth is reasoned to.

I am sure she also feels the same for me. We play the violin as feeling each other in the bottom of heart. I don't know how many of them in the hall could sense the similarity of our rhythm.

We speak, laugh, walk, eat, travel, hug, kissed and essentially loved each other. Her love was doing magic and making a magical world will eat all the days like a ferocious hungry animal.

Later, all the music classes get final days and get completed. I begin to work as a pizza delivery boy. She begins to be with her father, who needs perfect caring and started working as a typist. It all goes well more than I expect. She introduces me to her father. He was in the middle and final stage of ALS. He can't speak. But he smiled at me when she introduces me to him. I looked at the background behind him; it was all surmounted by books. It was nearly like a mini-library. I had a coffee together with him. After a few minutes of presence, he rolled his wheelchair to his room and keep the door open. The wheelchair is very special as it is manufactured for such diseased people. It has a cellular phone attachment. He could not speak but at least make some sound to his daughter to indicate his emergency situation.

Then we start to walk on the seashore together. We hold hands. The scene is very perfect, like a movie scene. The only problem is my pizza delivery uniform. But she did not mind that. Her mind is feeding something. It must be something terrible as her face demonstrate.

I asked her, "What you're going through?" She says nothing. I know she is hiding something from me, and also, I know she can't do that for long.

We walking on the seashore, the sea is speaking through waves, and behind the sea, the sun moving along with us. There is perfect silence between us as I understand that she was oscillating something in her mind. After some more walk steps, she begins, "I don't know what I am making in my mind. I lost my mother soon after my seventh birthday. And I still miss her, though my father tried a lot. He also misses her. I am sure he will miss her more than I do. He once told me she was the most beautiful woman he ever met. And now along with the feeling for my mother, there is the addition of feeling for my father". As she was speaking and I was becoming emotional, the walking speed gets slower. I don't know what to say in reply. I hold her hand tightly, then little. She had tears coming over her eyes. She looked at me with the same crying eyes and said, "I have nothing but only you as my happiness and the hope for my life". She cleaned the tears that flow over her face. Her last words make me cry along with her. I get no comments to tell her. I just nodded like yes, along with tears on my eyes and a smile on my lips. She kissed me. That kiss consists of love, hope, happiness and completely everything of her. That kiss lasted for a long time than usual.

• • •

Chapter 11

On the same night, I put my body on a terrace. The music is playing as usual—the violin is near to me. I was smoking today after long months of gap. Though I hate to smoke even today, I need it as the brain bears a complex emotion in enlarged quantity. So I was smoking and staring at the sky full of stars.

The complex emotions are due to her. It is the day, I think, which become the worst day because of her. I love her but don't know whether to continue or not. I know she was the girl who brings light, happiness and hopes to my life. In the meantime, I was also like that for her. I never want her to lift life to the next level. But I need to go on the path of pursuing my dream life.

I have many dreams in my life, like making a great

music band, composing music for movies, and finally, I want to lead a happy life with peace. I want to become a success as much as to give a Ted Talk. In simple, I like the life of a celebrity. I want to achieve in the field of music.

It's all one part of the mind that arguing with the other. The other is arguing like "How can you leave your loved one?". It also adds like I should be with her and heal all her problems as she believes me to do that. Or at least to be near her as a one and only happiness, in-between all her bad stuff. I should not break the hope she had on me. She has no other than me to have as a solution. I want to be with her, hold her hands and walk on the seashore again and again until death calls us. That is all she needs from me and nothing at all.

These are the two between which my all neurons are oscillating with a lot of confusion. I want to cry, but I can't. The love and dreams are bombarding with each other in the brain, and the heavy loss, blood, and sorrow are coming out as a cloud of smoke. I smoked, again and again; little tears gave birth in my eyes. The pain goes through by the heart is like unnumbered atomic bombs explode in the same place at the exact second.

I was in a situation similar to someone who asked, "Which eye of yours is hated by you?". I need both eyes. Both my dream and the love of my life. But fate has written for me to leave one to get the another.

I decide to choose the one and stop the oscillation

from going inside my head. I know at initial that the choice I choose will hurt both of us for sure. If I live with her and leaving all the passion towards love, we live together with a lack of money and finally die in poverty. We may happy for each other's presence but not at all for the other things. If I go in the path of holding my passion, it will hit at each other for the loss of each other.

Both the choice is going to give pain for her, and it is entirely because of me. I don't want to present near her and make it worst again and again. I need her to be happy, no matter with her. All I need is a good, comfortable life for her. The sound and comfort life may make her forget me and make her have a complete presence of happiness.

Chapter 12

Last night I cried, cried and slept in crying. So I wake up very late in the morning. As the first thought me the yesterday's decision. Again the tears are generating. I tell myself I have no other way to stop hurting her. This decision is going to hurt her but not long as the other choice does.

There was a missed call from the place where I am working nowadays. I hurried up as putting all my emotion down. I get dressed in a uniform and go to work.

While travelling, all my mind is speaking about aborting yesterday's decision. I convince myself not to do that. I don't know how to tell that to her. My brain starts to visualize the possible events if I speak about my oscillation and decision. I don't want her to cry or go through any killing pain before me. I don't wish to in my absence, but I have no other choice for her goodness.

I have no guts feeling to tell and convince to leave me, and it will never come, I know. So I don't want to meet her, message her or speak to her. All I want is to leave her without making any sense to not make it a tragic day for both of us.

My mobile is ringing again. I beg not to be her. But it was her. I don't know whether to pick it or not. One half of mine is telling to choose and the other to not. Unfortunately, I picked up. I show that I am not interested in talking. She was speaking about meeting me in the evening. I say just okay and ask her what's for more to talk about? I am sure this itself enough to break her heart into pieces. She said she had another call and end the call. She did like that because she doesn't have to answer my cruel question or to my emotions in my words. After she hangs the call, I feel sorry for her. And this is the reason for my decision. That I can't bear her pain. I need her to be happy every day, which I could not give her.

I put my mobile phone in silence as I know she will call me to check I am okay. I start to concentrate on my work. But memories and the future which I planned to happen are comes like a moving picture in mind. It always hurt. To avoid it, I tried to concentrate on work and the conversation with the people near me.

She has called many times, but I haven't picked up.

• • •

My heart is continuously asking me to talk with her, but I will not.

It becomes more than evening, but the sadness about the future accommodates me with great intensity. There is again a call coming from her. I picked up to tell her to stop calling me. I ask her with fake rudeness bidding my crying, "What?" She speaks about my silence and avoidance to her with the vibrant mix of weeping, angry, and irritation.

I can't reply to her as I was engaged in pushing down my emotions. At one point, She stopped speaking and wait for my words. As I have not left any comments, we make silent for some minutes.

And finally, I hang the call and put my mobile on aeroplane mode. That night I slept as I hugged the violin and some music for a long time.

Chapter 13

The morning is precisely like yesterday's morning. I turn off the aeroplane mode. It suddenly shows the message which indicates that she had tried to reach me a lot of times. I question myself, "Why did you call her?" I replied from another part of the mind, "I don't know actually; maybe I do unconsciously."

I put all my mind again into rushing to work. She makes two or three missed calls while I was bathing. I know how much I am hurting her. And I don't know whether she knows I, too, have the pain – much more than her. If she doesn't know that, she will cry for that also. So I need to show that I will be happy without her or only without her. That is the reason I was not making any contact with her.

I start working. I put her number on the blocklist,

stopping her from calling me and looking after her life in a better way. I made a completely fake happy status in WhatsApp, which will be why she left me and made her life best and best, or at least better without me.

And it was the days when I make only unrealistic happiness and hide a sadness that is rooting deeply inside me everywhere. It has been five days, no sign of contact from her or no way for her to contact me. Precisely at the next day, while I was looking at some video in which a girl and boy playing the violin, it makes me go back to the old days where we have only love without a distance.

On the same day, in the noon, as I was working in the pizza restaurant, she comes there. I show like she is no one for me. She also does the same. Real love will always be accompanied by an equal level of ego on showing love. She did that as she was aware I need that, and not from her bottom of heart. I don't know whether she knows that I am showing such ignorance, not even from the heart. She makes a bill for one pizza, but she eats a tiny pinch of it, a slice only. She leaves a letter with words to convey that I need to come to the beach for five minutes in the evening.

I decide to go and put a full stop to everything between us. We both stand as locating the sea. I never say a word so as to not extend the time of giving her pain. She starts, "What's happening between?" I said, "Nothing". After she heard that unmindful word, she kept to herself for a while. After few more minutes, I

* * *

have told all the things I am going through and all the decisions I have made. While speaking, I have never looked at her. After she heard all the things I said, she didn't say anything. She waved a bye and left. I can sense the cry on that bye which she tries to hide. I shouted, "I am going out of this country next week. So end all this drama". I hate myself heavily for using the word drama but can't able to change it. She did not react and kept walking.

Chapter 14

The silence she had given to me is most painful, like having a fire inside a heartbeat. She must shout at me, scold me, and fight or at least try to tear my shirt. Her silence is making me guilty. She should express her pain in any form on me. But she did not, and it made me hate myself more and more.

I start to cry every night and wear a mask of being alright in the daytime. I loved her, looked for a future with her, and believed that my life is impossible without her. But I betrayed her love, care for me.

I realized that I may get all my dream and made a super wondering life. But it is not possible to have an angel hearted girl like her to be beside my life. As I was crying with wetting the pillow, the heart again taught me that you can't live without her. So I called her to ask her sorry and fix her as girl who not get any pain of love. But the mobile call did not connect to her as she made her mobile dead by switching it off.

I thought like she was bearing the unbearable pain of love. She killed her mobile to avoid herself from trying to call me and betray herself again and again.

The pain of love is the most painful pain in the world from which no one escaped. And I go through it. I haven't loved anyone like her, and also, no one loved me like her. "But how my heart makes me leave her" is the thing that tears my mind again and again. I need to leave her only for good, and there is no selfishness. I want her to be happy without bearing any pain from anyone. But, if I live with her, I will be in the pain of leaving my dream somewhere, and that pain made her have wounds. And to save both of us from future pain, I am taking hard steps now, which I believe will be good.

I haven't heard a call or message from her since the day we met. I want to learn what she was going through. I prayed God not put any pain into her and to make her stronger to bear the pain given by me.

I hope she was not going to come back to my home. I compromise my heart not to contact her still she not make a try to contact me. It happens like she was going to be completely absent from my life. That is what I wish to happen. But it is paining now. We randomly like to happen some events, but we cannot look at the consequences or emotions of those events.

It has been a few days, and there is no sign of her.

* * *

And I also am hiding all this while. But one morning of sleeplessly crying light, she comes again to my home.

She comes nearly to my room while I was fixing my violin. I have kept my room already locked to avoid distractions from outside. She called me with severe crying. I was shocked on crying. As I could not look at her face, I stopped crying to open the door for her. I ask, "what?" from inside. She answers with a question with crying, "Why are you doing like this? What is the mistake I have made for you?. You are the one who creates a love, hope, future and makes me feel I can't live without you." All the words of her are falling like a rumble of thunder inside me. I cried back, "Please leave me… that is only good for both of us." She wiped all her tears and said clearly, "I am not going to come into your life. And understand you are the one and only reason for the pain I am going through and the ruin of our beautiful love," she struck in her words, "I know you love me. And also you love music. But I never thought that you compare the music and me. And put me away and took the music in your hands". She fades away from there without hearing my words. That night is the most soul firing pain I gone through.

Chapter 15

It was the day I am getting out of this country. Can't able to tell I forget her or I still remember her. I have packed all my things and try to leave the memories I made with her, though I know it not possible. I packed my clothes and take all the documents necessary to leave the border of the country.

It was exactly five minutes before I got out of my residence. I hear the sound of the calling bell. I can't be able to put what the feeling had created by the calling bell. It is somehow a mix of curiosity, fear and the addition of some other emotions. I unlock my door to make a view. It was her. It was like a natural disaster happening to a peaceful Buddha temple. It is like a complete turnover of all of mine. I was entirely shocked as much as to forget to call her inside or give any sign. She enters with the same rights she deserves. I never say anything, and she too.

I check all the things that I packed. She stands near me and just looks over her mobile and at all. But I could sense the tear that filling her eyes. But I don't want to make it as any conversation to not mess up the situation or my mood. The taxi arrived, I entered, and she also entered, which I didn't accept. I feared that she also going to come along with me. Finally, my voice did show up to ask her anything.

We arrived at the airport. I make all the formalities to leave this country. And she just being present like someone to make bye in my departure.

As I have ten minutes for my flight. I like to make a smooth conversation with her without any hardness to both of us. But as I know, it is not possible to do. Yes, love is always the most pleasurable magic, but, in the meantime, making an absence of the same love is killing pain in every nook of heart cells.

We stand near to near, without any word. Occasionally see one another and sometimes make eye contact, which creates love like in the old days and produces pain in both of our eyes.

My heart is asking me to say sorry. And it was correct. I was the one who had built hope, love, happiness and all inside her. And I am the same one who destroyed all that with an evil heart. I am the only reason for both of our pain.

After a complex of thoughts, I asked her for forgiveness. She looks at me with a lot of pain, like seeing my pain as a reflection of her pain. I know we both begging for not a separation and only for closeness as much as possible. But though I look for intimacy, I need a departure for her peaceful life. My sorry doesn't make her speak anything, but it makes the tears fall down from her eyebrows, which she cleaned without showing to me. And it's her who endure pain for me. But I don't want to give her pain at all by having her in one hand and another with the toughest dream. And finally, the departure comes for everything when the flight arrives.

As I was becoming invisible in the elevator, she waves a bye for me with teary eyes. I am sure I have departed from the place and from her memories, or at least not from her fingerprint on my violins, signs of her kiss, hug, laugh, smile, and finally, the angry tears of her.

Chapter 16

I try to put down the emotions I had at the travel in the flight. I arrived in a new country. I searched for the person John sir had told me about. It was Mathew. He arranged everything like residence, food and all other necessities. I practice in the piano, violin, guitar, and other musical instruments again and again. I also learned to use the computer for increasing the quality of my music. It becomes nearly more than a year for me to set a perfect crew to create original music. If John sir thought he can also do that for me, he didn't do that as I have to grow and build the basement of my career on my own.

Even after making a perfect crew and contact, I procrastinated on the works as still some memories of her disturbing me. I try of forgetting the past, which is the most challenging thing for me. I go and look for different people, different places. That helps me to distract from her and the guilt of the pain I made for. That also helps me in making a piece of new music and new tunes.

It takes half a year to do my first album after I set my crew and album. It was produced by John sir. The song is about a man who tries to hide his own feelings from himself. And you know that man was exactly like me. The album is hit over everywhere. The level reached by the album is more than we expect. I get somewhat famous inside my small surrounding. There is a call from John sir, the friends of my orphanage and the music class.

I expect a call from her. If she heard the album, she could understand that the love I had for her and the love I am having for her is true to a fact. But unfortunately, no call from her. I can't have anything to predict that she would hear my album or not. I wished every call would be her, but she did not make any missed calls or messages. A significant part of my heart is praying for her presence, at least at minimum.

I become more depressed to be where I can feel like I have succeeded but lost her. I am seeking a single word – something good or bad about the album. I can compromise my heart that she has looked at it and understand something about the things my heart has gone through while leaving her away and not choosing to talk to me.

Chapter 17

It becomes finally four years of departure from her. I have made nearly eight albums and also composed a background score for one movie. I have achieved the life I dreamed of. I have crossed many girls, but everybody makes me remember the girl who loved me more. I occasionally miss her presence.

I have earned enough even to go for one year of vacation. I want to know how good she is doing now. I called her number, but it was useless. I don't know what to do. I search for what to do. I don't even know whether she married or not. What about her father.

After a long time, one of my friends in that music class contacts me. He wished me for the success I had. With a heavy hesitation, I tried to ask him about her life. He said she had cut off all the contact. And he also tells the bad news of her father's death. I couldn't ask more about her after hearing about her father's death.

I think about the pain she got due to her one and only father dying. I can't even imagine it completely. I can't even imagine that she is alone. I feel wrong about it for not being near to her as support. Again I can't sleep that night and cry over and over.

As the days grow with much loveless time in my life. The reoccurrence of the same initial love intensity for her. Every day, especially the night, come to ask for me to go in search of her.

It is all okay to go in search of her again. But if my presence near her, may hurt her again. She may have a family or at least someone else in her life. My presence may ruin her life again. And I hate that. So I avoid to go look for her.

But I can't hear my mind for long days. My heart is always asking me to go in search again and again. It asks me to check how she was.

Eventually, the love I had for her made me search for her after four to five years of breakup.

Chapter 18

I come back to my old house where I learn and practice most of the musical instruments. It had all the memories as if it happened yesterday. I love the nostalgic feel tended by the walls of the rooms. The cry she made outside my room and the cry I made inside the room all come in front of my eyes. The house is one of John sir's property. He must be busy, so there is no one to maintain it after my departure. So, I cleaned every nook of the room.

While cleaning, I look at the drawing of my face in the main door. The drawing is made with a white line, and it is very small. Nevertheless, it is the evidence of her presence here after I had departed. It blooms an unbearable smile inside my peripheral fluid.

I go to the music class, there was a lot of new faces.

· · ·

No one aware of who I was, but I was not concerned about that. As usual in the hall, all are waiting for John sir's presence. I also start to wait for them. John sir come in the same old car. He was surprised to see me. He has grown older with little more white hair. I tell him about the ongoing projects. He is really happy for me. He introduces me to everybody in his class. After thirty minutes of conversation with them, I move out from there. The opposite coffee shop where I propose to her has changed to some multicomplex. That change makes a slight disappointment in me.

With a great mix of fear and happiness, I get to her home. It was locked. I can't predict whether she is temporarily out or have gone off to the distance as much as to hide from me. I go and search on the beach where she usually loves to be. But there too no evidence of her presence. I search everywhere she could possibly be, but I can't get her. My heart is telling me that I have missed my soul with a crying tone. I want just to look at her smiling face, which I had ruined once upon a time.

I have full hope at the beginning that I will see her with happiness. But I can't even look at her single penny of presence. I start to go repeatedly to the same place again and again. The house is still locked. And I can't find her for a long and long time of the day.

And finally, I get into the mall where she is usually gone to purchase something along with her friends. I searched every shop on that ten floored mall. I become tired heavily with a sweating body and face.

• • •

The sudden sound of a birthday blaster makes my body jump in fear. I looked in the direction of the sound. A girl is celebrating her birthday. Near to the birthday girl, the girl I love the most is standing, wearing a broad smile of happiness. Her hand is held by someone who looks handsome and charming than me. She suddenly looked at me, so I hide beside one of the benches immediately. I think she has sensed my presence because she is coming in my direction, searching for me or for some other. The boy who holds her hands comes and takes her to her original position. They eat the cake. They may be a couple.

My heart is asking me to show my presence to her. But my mind is asking me to go away as I can see that her happiness is with someone else.

This time I go in the flow of mind. I start to fade away from there.

Chapter 19

As someone making a sound of my name, I stopped from fading away from there. It was her who called me. Her eyes have already half-filled with tears. I turned around with heavy emotions. I looked at her with a smile. I asked, "How are you?" She replied, "I'm okay. And you?" I tell with a smile "good".

She interrogates, "what are you doing here?". I tell the truth without consciousness "I come in search of you". Her eyes fill with tears as enough to get down. But she tries to make rude in her voice. "for what?" she questioned again.

"Just to find whether you're happy or not?"

"How such things come to your mind. After avoiding me for years and years?"

I can't be able to reply to her final question. I made

a facial emotion to dilate that question. I asked about the boy who holds her hands. She said that he was a cousin of her. That answer makes me give rebirth to the old self, which loves her unconditionally.

She could also sense what's happening inside me. I ask for her number. She answers again with the question, "for what".

"For what?" is the term I used to ruin the love between us. And she is now using the same thing on me. I tell her, "I'm sorry for everything I did. I agree all the mistakes are mine".

"So what?"

I couldn't speak.

She continued, "I know you will come in search of me again. Because you can't live without me. Actually, I have been waiting for this day to come".

I interrupted her, "I am still having the love for you. I cause pain for you and for myself. It's all because of the love I had for you".

"I know you still love me. But still, some wounds are causing pain inside."

"I am sorry for everything. Please… forgive me."

Both of our eyes were leaving out tears.

"No… I love you, but I can't believe you. How can I believe you that you will not break me again?!" her words hit me hard. "If you do that, I can bear that!"

"Just tell me what to do. Otherwise, give some punishment?" my tears falling over my cheeks.

"No, I don't want anything to do with you" those were her final words. She quickly ran away from there to not cry in public.

Chapter 20

I know the mistakes are mine and only mine. I started to wait for her as she did for me. She will come back one day, and we both explore the love as making everyone feel jealous of us. I believe love is pleasure, it is magic, and mostly it is powerful to do anything. I also think love will happen again between us, just like in the old days.

I come back to her as I could not live without her. She waits for me to come as she only lives with me. And so, she will soon come to me.

More than hope, magic and power, love is mad. So, it makes you do anything for the person you are insane about.

THE END

Acknowledgement

First of all, I thank myself for trying this. Second, I need to thank all my school and college friends who always shower love to my writings. They are the only reason I was motivated enough to write this book. Especially, I would like to thank my best friend, Maha Sakthi Vel, who has been with me since childhood. He was the only one who consistently shows a tremendous amount of interest in reading my writings.

Then, I extend my thanks to my mother, Uma Maheswari, who hates my writings, but still gives me an infinite amount of love. Then, my father, Manoharan who is the only reason for my knowledge, thinking, and creativity. I would also like to thank all the people out there who directly or indirectly became the reason for this book to been written.

Finally, but with much intensity, I thank Bumblebee Publishing for accepting my proposal and helping me make my dream come true and for also helping me turn my book into a beautiful read.

9 788819 494852